BASKETBALL
BREAKDOWN

BY JAKE MADDOX

text by
Val Priebe

STONE ARCH BOOKS
a capstone imprint

Jake Maddox JV Girls books are published by
Stone Arch Books
a Capstone imprint
1710 Roe Crest Drive
North Mankato, Minnesota 56003

www.mycapstone.com

Library of Congress Cataloging-in-Publication Data

Names: Maddox, Jake, author. | Priebe, Val, author.
Title: Basketball breakdown / by Jake Maddox ; text by Val Priebe.
Description: North Mankato, Minnesota : Stone Arch Books, a Capstone imprint,
    [2017] | Series: Jake Maddox JV girls | Summary: When eighth grade basketball
    player Shaena suffers a concussion in a game, she finds herself sidelined two
    weeks before the big game—and as she watches her team practice with the new
    freshman player, Shaena, who is used to being the star, starts to worry that by the
    time she recovers she will no longer be needed.
Identifiers: LCCN 2016012071| ISBN 9781496531667 (library binding) | ISBN
    9781496536761 (pbk.) | ISBN 9781496536808 (ebook pdf)
Subjects: LCSH: Basketball stories. | Teamwork (Sports)—Juvenile fiction. |
    Brain—Concussion—Juvenile fiction. | Competition (Psychology)—Juvenile
    fiction. | Self-confidence—Juvenile fiction. | CYAC: Basketball—Fiction.|
    Teamwork (Sports)—Fiction. | Brain—Concussion—Fiction. | Competition
    (Psychology)—Fiction. | Self-confidence—Fiction.
Classification: LCC PZ7.M25643 Bao 2017 | DDC 813.6 [Fic] —dc23
LC record available at https://lccn.loc.gov/2016012071

Art Director: Nathan Gassman
Designer: Kayla Rossow
Media Researcher: Morgan Walters
Production Specialist: Tori Abraham

Photo Credits:
Shutterstock: Aaron Amat, (basketball) 96, Angie Makes, design element, cluckva, design
element, Dan Kosmayer, (stick) 96, Derek Hatfield, design element, Eky Studio, design
element, irin-k, (soccer) 96, Lightspring, (volleyball) 96, Monkey Business Images, Cover

Printed in the United States of America in Stevens Point, Wisconsin.
009622F16

TABLE OF CONTENTS

CHAPTER 1
POST PROBLEMS. 5

CHAPTER 2
HARD HIT. 11

CHAPTER 3
SEEING STARS 21

CHAPTER 4
THE DIAGNOSIS. 29

CHAPTER 5
NOT FAIR. 35

CHAPTER 6
SIDELINED 43

CHAPTER 7
REPLACED 51

CHAPTER 8
TOUGH TALK. 59

CHAPTER 9
APOLOGIES 67

CHAPTER 10
REBOUND. 73

CHAPTER 11
BACK IN THE GAME. 81

POST PROBLEMS

FWEET!

Coach Riley's whistle cut through the noisy gym. "Water break!" she yelled.

Shaena Davis jogged to the sideline to get a drink. She shot an exhausted smile to Marisol King, her best friend and teammate, over the top of her water bottle.

"Phew!" said Marisol in between heavy breaths. "Coach is really working us today."

Shaena nodded. "We'll definitely be ready for our first game with Springfield tomorrow."

She could hardly wait to get back on the court. Shaena had spent half the summer at basketball camp and the other half practicing at the rec center up the street so she'd be ready for her eighth grade season. Even though she was the best post player on her team, the South Redford Tigers, she always wanted to be better.

"So, is Springfield any good?" a quiet voice asked.

Marisol and Shaena turned to see Jessie Bechtold next to them, grabbing her water bottle. Jessie had just transferred to South and was new to the team. She'd only played one season at her old school, so she was pretty new to basketball too.

Jessie had been pretty quiet their first few practices. Shaena felt like she hardly knew her, even though they were both playing post.

Marisol sighed. "Unfortunately, yeah," she replied. "They're pretty good."

"But they're not crazy good," added Shaena. "We're usually evenly matched, but I bet we'll get them this year."

"Everyone, bring it in!" Coach called.

The three girls quickly capped their water bottles and hustled over. The team gathered in center court around Coach Riley.

"Okay, let's work on our offense and defense," said Coach. "Remember, game speed. Practice like we play."

The team split into their usual groups. Shaena, Marisol, and Annie played offense first. Jessie, Christine, and Beth were on defense.

Marisol stood at the stop of the three-point arc with the ball. Christine lunged in for a steal, but Marisol dodged her and passed the ball to Annie.

Shaena sprinted to the free-throw line with her hands up. "Annie, ball!" she shouted.

Annie faked a pass back to Marisol and then snapped the ball to Shaena.

Up strong, use the backboard, Shaena told herself, repeating the layup advice from her summer camp coach. She dropped her right foot back and around Jessie, then spun past her. Dribbling once, she made the layup.

The shrill sound of Coach's whistle stopped the play. "Nice fake, Annie, and great job, Shaena!" yelled Coach. "Jessie, that's exactly what I want you to do, just give her a little more space."

Jessie gave a sharp nod. "Got it," she said.

On the next play, Jessie did just what Coach had told her to do. Shaena dropped her right foot back, ready to go in for the layup again. But as she turned to throw the ball, there was Jessie.

The other post player jumped, and the ball made a loud *thump* as it smacked into her hands. Jessie grabbed the ball from the air and hit the court, ready to make a move.

Shaena felt her cheeks turn red. A rookie had just blocked her shot!

Coach blew her whistle again. "Fantastic, Jessie! That was great defense!" she shouted.

"Yeah, nice block!" added Christine as she high-fived Jessie, who smiled shyly at all the attention.

"Shaena, that's a good move, but try to mix it up a little, okay?" said Coach Riley.

"Okay, Coach," agreed Shaena.

The drop step was her signature move, but Shaena scolded herself for using it twice in a row. She would have to switch things up in tomorrow's game to keep the Springfield defense guessing.

As Shaena got ready for another run-through, she watched the other post player more carefully. Although Jessie was new to basketball, she had some natural talent and was clearly getting better with each practice.

Shaena's stomach twisted. *Will I be sharing the spotlight?* she wondered.

CHAPTER 2

HARD HIT

Friday night, Shaena stood in front of the gym doors where she could hear muffled noises. The familiar flutter of butterflies rose in her stomach, making her feel queasy and excited at the same time. She always got these pregame jitters when she heard the loud chatter of the spectators and the upbeat warm-up music.

"Ready for our first game?" Marisol asked, coming up behind her.

Shaena smiled and gave a nod. "Ready."

The South Redford Tigers jogged out onto the court and started their warm-up routine. Shaena soon forgot her butterflies as she concentrated on perfecting her movements, reminding herself to hold her follow-through on her jump shot.

Eventually the clock wound down, and the music stopped. It was time for both teams to line up for the jump ball.

Shaena came to the center of the court. Because she was South's tallest player, she always jumped for the ball. But the Springfield player was even taller than Shaena. The two girls took their positions across from one another, facing toward their own baskets.

The referee checked to make sure all of the players were in position. Then he tossed the ball up in the air between Shaena and the Springfield post.

Shaena and the other player leaped up for the ball. Even though she was a couple of inches shorter, Shaena timed her jump better. She tipped the ball over her head back to Marisol.

South's fans cheered as Marisol took the ball and dribbled up the court. Shaena ran into position at the right side of the basket.

Just like they'd practiced, Shaena turned toward Marisol and held her right hand out, giving Marisol a target to pass to. The pass zinged into Shaena's hands. She brought the ball close to her chest, turned, aimed, and took the shot.

SWISH! The ball went cleanly through the hoop. Shaena had scored the first basket of the game!

"Way to go, Shaena!" someone cheered from the stands. Shaena grinned, immediately recognizing the voice — her mom had always been her biggest fan.

But Shaena quickly focused back on the game. Springfield's point guard had grabbed the ball and was dribbling back up the court, unfazed by South's fast start.

The Springfield post player took her spot near the basket, holding her arms above her head to get the attention of the point guard. Shaena got into a defensive position, moving just behind the other girl so that she'd be between her opponent and the basket.

The point guard passed to her right. The teammate faked a pass back to the point guard, who quickly passed to the post player.

Shaena brought her hands up, trying to protect the net. But she couldn't overcome her opponent's height this time. The other post player, tall as she was, simply turned, shot, and scored over Shaena's arms.

This is going be a tough one, Shaena thought as the ball fell through net.

The teams stayed neck-and-neck throughout the first quarter. They were both playing well — trading baskets, stealing passes, and making free throws when their players were fouled.

Although Springfield started to pull ahead in the second quarter, South wasn't about to give up. By halftime, the score was tied 30–30.

The girls gathered in the locker room at halftime, sweating but feeling good. Coach Riley went over plays she wanted to try in the second half to fight off Springfield's tough offense. Overall, though, she was happy with the team's performance.

"Great job, Tigers! You're keeping Springfield on their toes, and that's just what I like to see," she said. "One more half to go. Keep it up!"

As the team headed out of the locker room, Coach Riley took Shaena aside. "You've got three fouls, Shaena. Watch that. I don't want one of my best players out of the game."

"Got it, Coach," Shaena replied. She had two fouls left before she fouled out of the game completely, but she wasn't about to sit out the season's first game.

As soon as the teams took the court, Shaena could tell the second half was going to be rough. Springfield was still as fast as ever, but the South players were tired and starting to make mistakes. When Marisol made a rare bad pass, Springfield's point guard stole the ball for an easy layup. South was now down by three.

A few plays later, Shaena was once again playing defense behind the Springfield post player. Shaena crouched down behind the post, waiting for her to make a move.

You're not scoring this time, thought Shaena.

The other post player caught the pass from the point guard. She still had her back to Shaena. Shaena shot her arm out and around in an attempt to steal the ball. But as she reached to swat the ball, the other player turned suddenly. Shaena's hand bumped into the girl's arm.

FWEEET! The referee blew his whistle and raised a closed fist in the air. "Foul!"

Shaena let out a frustrated sigh. She had just picked up her fourth foul.

Springfield made the inbound pass and went in for another layup. Christine tried to block the shot, but she moved too slowly. The ball fell smoothly into the net.

With the ball in South's possession, Coach Riley signaled the referee for a time-out. The team quickly hustled over to the sideline.

"Okay, Tigers, get focused and catch your breath," said Coach when everyone had gathered by her. "Springfield is staying energized, so we need to play smart and not wear ourselves out."

The girls nodded. Many were sucking in deep breaths, but thanks to her practice and conditioning over the summer, Shaena was still feeling good.

Coach turned to Shaena. "Shaena, you're close to fouling out. Do I need to bring in Jessie?" Usually, Coach pulled players with four fouls so that the team wouldn't risk losing a player they might need in the very last minutes of the game.

"You have to keep me in, Coach," Shaena pleaded. "I've got energy to spare. I promise I'll be more careful."

Coach Riley nodded. "All right. Keep your heads in the game, ladies, and let's take back the court. Now, hands in the middle."

Shaena squished next to Marisol and Annie as the team gathered in and stacked their hands.

"One, two, three —" yelled Coach.

"Go Tigers!" the girls shouted.

The teams got back into position. Annie stood outside of the thick black line that marked the edge of the court, ready to make the inbound pass. The referee tossed her the ball, and Annie immediately flicked it to Marisol, who bolted down the court with renewed energy.

Shaena faked to the left, breaking free of her defender. "Mari!" she shouted, raising her hand.

The ball flew into Shaena's hands. She pivoted and took the shot, but the ball hit the front of the rim and bounced off hard.

Shaena sprinted after the rebound with the Springfield post right beside her. Each girl dived to the floor and slid across the hardwood on their stomachs, scrambling for the ball. But as they both reached for it, Shaena hesitated.

I can't risk picking up that fifth foul! she thought.

Shaena hung back, and the other girl got her hand on the ball first.

As the two girls rushed to their feet, the other post player quickly pulled the ball toward herself. Her elbows shot out to the sides.

Before Shaena had time to react, the Springfield post's elbow collided with her temple. Blinding pain exploded in Shaena's head as she lost sight of the ball and fell to the hardwood floor.

CHAPTER 3

SEEING STARS

The Springfield post passed the ball to her teammate, but Shaena remained on the floor, dazed and holding her head. Bright stars clouded her vision. Her ears were ringing. She tried to stand up, but a surge of dizziness kept her on the ground.

FWEET! The referee blew his whistle, stopping play. He waved Coach Riley out onto the floor.

"I'm okay, Coach," said Shaena as the coach crouched next to her.

"Let's get you off the court so I can make sure," Coach replied, motioning for Marisol to come over.

"You all right?" Marisol whispered as she helped Shaena stand up.

"I'm fine, really," Shaena whispered back, even though her head was buzzing. "Everyone's just making a big deal out of nothing."

Marisol and the coach each took one of Shaena's arms to steady her. The crowd clapped as they walked toward the bench.

Shaena flopped down onto the wooden seat while Coach signaled Jessie to take Shaena's place. Marisol shot a worried look at Shaena before joining Jessie on the court.

Coach Riley kneeled in front of Shaena. "Follow my finger with just your eyes," she instructed.

Shaena did as she was told, but it was hard to concentrate. She hardly noticed that her mom had come down from the bleachers and now knelt by Coach Riley.

Coach frowned and lowered her hand. "Shaena, I'm concerned that you might have a concussion."

"What?" exclaimed Shaena, immediately wincing at the bolt of pain that shot through her head. "No, I can go back in."

Coach shook her head. "No way. You need to be seen by a doctor," she said. "I can't let you play until you've been given a clean bill of health."

"But, Coach," said Shaena, nearly in tears. She wasn't sure if the tears were from the throbbing in her head or the fact she was getting sidelined in the first game of the season. Maybe both. "There are only two more minutes left in the game. Please!"

"Shaena, Coach Riley is right," said Shaena's mom, taking hold of her hand. "No more arguing."

"You can sit with the team for the rest of the game," Coach continued, "but then you need to go to a doctor."

"Fine," mumbled Shaena. She couldn't muster up the energy to argue. Her stomach was starting to feel a little upset too.

"I'll call Dr. Lee," Mom said. She stood up and pulled out her cell phone. "Hopefully she can see you tonight."

As her mom left the gym to make the call, Shaena stayed on the bench and tired to focus on the game. But it was hard with the fuzzy pain pressing against the inside of her head.

They were down to the final minutes of the game. Beth had managed a quick layup after the injury time-out, so now they were only down by three. If they could get the ball to Marisol, who was a good three-point shooter, South would have a chance to tie.

Come on, Shaena thought desperately.

Back and forth the teams went, but the three-point difference in the score didn't budge. With just five seconds left, Springfield took a shot.

CLANG!

The shot bounced off the rim. Jessie jumped for the rebound as Marisol sprinted for the three-point line on the other end.

Get it, Jessie! Shaena pleaded silently.

But Jessie didn't come down with the ball; a Springfield player did. The opposing player held onto the ball while the last seconds disappeared.

BUZZZZ!

Shaena sighed unhappily. The game was over, and South was still behind by three.

* * *

The disappointed South players filed into the locker room. Still a little dazed, Shaena walked with Marisol. She'd never imagined the first game ending like this.

Coach Riley was the last to come into the room. "No sad faces!" she told the team. "Look, I get it. We lost a game we fought really hard to win.

I don't like to lose either. But we played so well! I'm excited to see what you ladies will do this season."

With the coach's after-game talk complete, the girls were dismissed. As Shaena stood in front of her locker and changed back into her street clothes, she heard Coach talking.

"Great job tonight, Jessie," Coach said. "It's tough to get thrown into the game when your teammate has been hurt, but you did just fine."

"Thanks, Coach!" said Jessie.

Shaena let out an angry huff. *I would've been able to grab that rebound. And I would've been able to get the ball to Marisol,* she thought. *We should be celebrating a win tonight.*

She was stuffing her uniform into her bag when Marisol plopped down beside her on the bench.

"Hey. How do you feel?" Marisol asked quietly.

"I'm fine," Shaena insisted. She was getting frustrated. Why wouldn't anyone believe her?

"That was a hard hit you took," said Marisol. "I saw that girl rubbing her elbow afterward."

"Yeah, now Coach thinks I have a concussion," Shaena admitted. "I can't play until I get cleared by a doctor."

"Whoa, really?" said Marisol. "I'm so sorry, Shaena. But maybe Coach is wrong. Maybe the doctor will tell you you're totally fine."

"Maybe," said Shaena. She hung her aching head and reached for her sneakers.

Marisol let out a long breath. Then she put a hand on Shaena's shoulder, stood up, and walked back to her own locker.

At least I'll have an answer tonight, thought Shaena. She closed her eyes for a moment against the bright lights of the locker room. *But what if it's not the one I want to hear?*

CHAPTER 4

THE DIAGNOSIS

Inside the doctor's office, Shaena sat on the exam table as Dr. Lee looked her over. The doctor had agreed to stay late, so Shaena and her mom had gone straight from the school to the clinic.

"And then her elbow just sort of hit the side of my head," Shaena finished explaining.

"Did you see stars or spots of light in front of your eyes?" asked Dr. Lee. She shined a tiny flashlight into Shaena's eyes as she asked questions.

"Yeah," admitted Shaena. The light was doing nothing for her headache. "But only for a second."

"I see," said Dr. Lee. "Do you have a headache now? Do you feel sick to your stomach?"

The sick feeling in Shaena's stomach had faded, so she replied honestly, "Nope. Not anymore."

"But you did feel sick, and you still have a headache?" Dr. Lee pressed.

Shaena looked away. "Yeah," she said quietly.

Dr. Lee put the flashlight down. "Shaena, I'm afraid you have a minor concussion," she said. Shaena started to protest, but the doctor held up a hand. "It might not have seemed like a big hit, but concussions can happen from small hits too."

The doctor went over to her computer and printed something out. She grabbed the papers and handed them to Shaena.

"Those printouts have info on concussions — what it is, symptoms, and so on," Dr. Lee explained. "But basically a concussion is a bruise on your brain that happens when you hit your head. There's a little bit of room between the brain and the skull.

A hard hit can cause the brain to move and bump against the skull, which causes the bruise."

Shaena frowned as she glanced at the papers. *How could a tiny hit make my brain move?* she wondered.

"One of the first things that happens when you get a concussion is you see little spots of light in front of your eyes," continued Dr. Lee. "Then you'll have a headache. Sometimes people feel like they might throw up. Some people get confused. Other people black out completely."

Shaena sighed impatiently. "Okay, but I don't feel sick, I didn't black out, and I'm not confused."

Dr. Lee gave a sympathetic smile. "You don't have a major concussion, so you only have a few of the symptoms. But you're still injured. You'll need to follow my instructions if you don't want to be out of basketball any longer than you already need to be."

Out of basketball? Shaena's jaw dropped. "What? You can't be serious."

"Shaena," her mom warned. "Listen to Dr. Lee."

Shaena closed her mouth and waited for the doctor to continue.

"You'll likely have a headache for a few days," Dr. Lee said. "Because of that, you might have some trouble concentrating in school. So I want you to rest this weekend — no computer or TV, okay?"

"Okay," replied Shaena, trying to hold back tears. Those instructions felt like a prison sentence!

"I'll also write a note to keep you out of gym class — and basketball — for all of next week," finished Dr. Lee.

"A week?" Shaena exclaimed. "A whole *week*?"

"At least a week," corrected Dr. Lee. "And that's if you follow all of my instructions."

"But I can't miss basketball for a whole week!" insisted Shaena. She couldn't stop the tears from falling now. How could she be out for that long? It was just a little bump on the head!

"I know this is upsetting," said Dr. Lee. "But I can't budge on this — this is your brain we're talking about. Come and see me a week from today, and I'll see how you're doing then."

"Thank you, Dr. Lee," said Shaena's mom. "We appreciate you staying late to see us."

Dr. Lee nodded. "Any time."

Feeling numb, Shaena silently walked out of the clinic with her mom. Once they were in the car and buckled up, she turned to her mom.

"Maybe we should get a second opinion or something," Shaena suggested.

Mom shook her head. "Sorry, honey," she said. "I know this is tough."

Shaena sighed and looked out the car window. She felt a buzz in her backpack. It was a text from Marisol: *Did u go to the dr? R u ok?*

Tears welled up in Shaena's eyes again. There were a couple of text messages from her other teammates, but Shaena just shut off her phone, put it back into her backpack, and closed her eyes.

CHAPTER 5

NOT FAIR

The next morning, Shaena woke up with a growling stomach as the smell of pancakes and bacon drifted up from the kitchen. She stretched in bed and smiled before the dull pain in her head reminded her of everything that had happened last night. Suddenly, she wasn't so hungry anymore.

After tossing on a sweatshirt, she walked downstairs to find Marisol sitting at the kitchen table. Mom was flipping pancakes at the stove. Confused, Shaena looked down at her cell phone in her hand. There were no new text messages from Marisol.

"Hey, Shaena!" said Marisol brightly. "Good morning!"

"Hey, Mari," replied Shaena, not entirely sure what was going on.

Mom turned from flipping pancakes and smiled. "Good morning, honey," she said.

"Morning," Shaena replied slowly.

Mom put a few more pancakes on an already full plate, switched off the stove, and set the plate on the table before walking over to Shaena. She looked closely into Shaena's eyes, brushing a stray strand of hair out of her face. "How does your head feel this morning?" she asked.

"Fine. I don't know. It . . . it hurts a little," Shaena admitted.

"Do you want to take anything?" asked Mom.

"I don't know," Shaena said again, feeling a little annoyed. She still felt fuzzy with sleep, and she was trying hard to remember inviting Marisol over for breakfast.

Did I text her back last night? Shaena wondered. Her stomach twisted. *What if this is the some of the confusion Dr. Lee mentioned last night? What if my concussion is worse than everyone thought?*

Mom must've noticed Shaena's confused expression. "Oh! I forgot to tell you last night after all of the excitement," she said. "I invited Marisol over for breakfast. I thought you might need a little cheering up."

Excitement? thought Shaena. *Last night was not exciting.*

"I bet you'd feel better if you ate something," her mom continued. "And Marisol, don't wait for Shaena. Dig in!"

With a grin, Marisol happily pulled three pancakes onto her plate along with several pieces of bacon.

"Hey," Shaena said again as she sat down across from Marisol. There was already a plate and a large glass of orange juice waiting for her.

"Hello!" Marisol mumbled through a full mouth. She gave a big, goofy grin stuffed with pancakes.

Shaena laughed despite the pain in her head. Her friend always knew how to make her feel better. Then, with jolt of guilt, Shaena remembered that she'd never responded to Marisol's text message.

"About last night, sorry I —" she began.

Marisol interrupted her. "Don't worry about not texting back," she said, swallowing her mouthful of pancakes. "I know you didn't feel well. I just wanted to let you know I was thinking about you."

Shaena gave her a half smile. "I'm sorry," she said, apologizing anyway. "Thank you. I should have responded."

Marisol waved away Shaena's apology. Then, Shaena's stomach let out a loud growl. The girls looked at each other and burst out laughing.

"Pancake time!" Mom announced, laughing too.

* * *

After breakfast, Shaena and Marisol were sleepy with their full stomachs. They lay on the couch listening to their favorite radio station.

"So . . . what did the doctor say?" Marisol asked quietly.

Shaena let out a loud sigh. She had been trying not to think about Dr. Lee's diagnosis. "She said that I have a minor concussion. I can't play basketball for at least a week."

Marisol cringed. "Oh, man. A whole week?"

"Yeah," replied Shaena. "I have to sit out of gym class too. *And* I still have this headache."

"That girl did hit you pretty hard, but you've taken hits to the head before," Marisol said, confused. "It's not like you got knocked out. How is this time different?"

"Beats me," said Shaena with a shrug. "Although Dr. Lee said you don't have to get knocked out to get a concussion."

"But you'll be back for the game against North in a couple of weeks, right?" asked Marisol after a few seconds of silence. "They won state last year — we need you!"

"I hope so," said Shaena.

"This is so unfair!" cried Marisol. "I mean, Christine played all last year with a sprained finger. And I get my ankle taped. Why is your injury such a big deal?"

"Dr. Lee says it's because it's my brain," explained Shaena. She picked at the pillow she held in her lap. "I just wish everyone didn't think I was so weak. I don't want to let the team down."

"Oh, Shaena!" Marisol exclaimed, sitting up with a start. "You're not letting anyone down!"

Shaena winced at Marisol's volume.

"Sorry," her friend continued, lowering her voice. "You're not. Seriously. You just need to rest. The team will be fine — but it's a good thing we have Jessie in the meantime!"

Shaena's stomach dropped at the mention of the new post player. "Um, yeah. I guess you're right," she replied. "Hey, I think I'm going to go back to sleep for a while. My head hurts."

"Oh . . ." said Marisol. "Okay. I'll just talk to you later, then."

"Yeah, okay," mumbled Shaena. "See you later."

Marisol stood up to leave, and Shaena wrapped herself in a blanket, trying not to think about Jessie taking her place on the court. If only she had just kept playing instead of lying there holding her head.

CHAPTER 6

SIDELINED

Monday morning at school, Shaena walked quickly down the hallway. She passed several of her teammates, who all waved to her. They looked like they wanted to ask how she was doing, but Shaena just gave a half-hearted wave and darted into her classroom before anyone could talk to her.

First period had just started, and already she could feel the headache that had stuck with her all weekend starting behind her eyes. After Marisol had left Saturday, Shaena had spent her time either lying in bed or lying on the couch, bored and miserable.

It's a good thing we have Jessie! Marisol had said. Shaena couldn't seem to stop hearing those words.

After suffering through the school day, Shaena walked into the gym before practice. She found Coach Riley and handed her Dr. Lee's note.

"That's what I was afraid of," Coach said after she'd read the slip of paper. "How do you feel?"

"Fine," replied Shaena, tired of answering the same question. "Can I stay for practice?"

Coach checked the note again. "Yes," she said slowly. "You can watch and learn our new play so you're ready to jump in when you're healed."

Shaena grinned.

"But," continued Coach in a stern voice, "that means no basketball — no dribbling, no running, no cheering. You're just watching. Got it?"

Shaena let out a loud sigh. "Got it."

"Good," said Coach. "For now, take it easy on the bench. If you feel unwell or need anything, just let me know."

Shaena nodded and sat down with a heavy thud, suddenly in a bad mood. She expected her mom to baby her but not Coach Riley.

Soon the locker room door banged open, and the team spilled out into the gym. Everyone was laughing and talking and ready for another practice.

Coach blew her whistle. Shaena felt a dull throb of pain in her head at the shrill sound, but she walked to the huddle with the rest of the team.

"We have a lot to get through before Thursday's game," began Coach Riley, "so just a couple of quick things and then we'll get started."

Coach gently patted Shaena's shoulder. "As you know, Shaena took a hard hit at the end of Friday's game. She's suffered a minor concussion, so she'll be sitting out until she heals up," she told the team.

Shaena's teammates voiced their shock with shouts of: "No!" and "Poor Shaena!" Immediately, Shaena felt even worse. She *was* letting her team down. Now she felt guilty and annoyed.

"She'll be back soon, we hope," Coach said over the chatter. "In the meantime, Jessie, you'll have to step up."

Jessie gave a nod and shot Shaena a sympathetic look. Shaena just studied a scuffmark on the floor.

Coach clapped her hands. "Now, let's work on the three-person weave," she instructed.

The team hustled into three lines under the basket for the drill. Shaena silently walked back to the bench on the sideline to watch.

Soon, the players were sweating and breathing hard as they worked to perfect their skills. The frustrated feeling grew in the pit of Shaena's stomach as she watched her teammates. *I'd give anything to be out there right now*, she thought.

After the team was done with the weave drill, Coach Riley set up the new play. Instead of Shaena in the post, though, Jessie took the position.

Jealousy and fear surged through Shaena. Jessie seemed to understand the play on the first try.

It was a twist on the traditional give-and-go, a move where a player passed the ball and then ran to the basket to be ready to receive it again. The play seemed specifically designed for Jessie and her hook shot from the middle of the lane.

The team ran the play until everyone had it down. Then Coach blew her whistle, and the girls stopped.

A loose ball rolled over toward Shaena as the team prepared for another drill. Half of the players were lined up along one long side of the court, with the other half of the team on the other side.

Shaena immediately recognized the exercise — a fast-break continuous three-on-two drill that Coach Riley called Guts and Glory.

The drill was fast-paced and fun — and it was Shaena's favorite. Now she could only sit and watch.

For the second time in just a few days, Shaena fought back tears. She looked down at the ball by her feet. *Technically, Coach never said I couldn't shoot the ball*, she reasoned.

Without another thought, Shaena grabbed the ball and defiantly walked over to a side basket.

Thunk. Swish. Bounce.

Shaena threw a short shot off the backboard and into the net. The movement and the *thunk* of the ball bouncing on the floor jarred Shaena's head. But the sounds of the drill happening behind her made her more determined. She grabbed the ball again.

Thunk. Swish. Bounce.

Thunk. Swish. Bounce.

"Shaena!" shouted a voice.

Shaena looked over her shoulder. Coach Riley was running toward her. Her teammates had stopped the drill and were staring at her.

"Shaena, give me the ball," Coach said crossly. "I'm sorry, but I can't let you shoot. I realize I didn't say that earlier, but you should know better — no basketball-related activities until you've been cleared by your doctor. If you can't follow those rules, I can't let you stay for practice."

Shaena reluctantly held out the ball. "Sorry, Coach," she mumbled. "It won't happen again."

The coach gave Shaena another warning look but took the ball and returned to the center court. Soon the team was running Guts and Glory again — without Shaena.

Shaena sat back down on the bench and waited for the end of practice, grumpier than ever. The occasional looks of sympathy from her teammates only made things worse.

Finally Coach Riley told the team she'd see them at tomorrow's practice. Shaena felt relieved for the first time in her life that basketball was over for the day.

As she stood to leave, Marisol waved to her and called, "Shaena! Hey, Shaena!"

But Shaena pretended not to hear. Instead she walked as fast as her aching head would allow through the locker room and away from her team.

REPLACED

Thursday's game was across town at Rockford Junior High. On the way there, Shaena sat in the back of the bus with Marisol, Annie, and the rest of the team, who were laughing and joking.

Shaena had a hard time joining in. Her mind was on the past two practices. They'd gone a little better. She had helped Coach Riley review the team's shooting statistics, and she'd read up on old plays and strategies. But it still hurt to see her teammates practice new plays without her.

Worse, Jessie was getting better at playing post. She was looking more comfortable with the team, too, easily chatting with Marisol, Christine, and Annie between drills.

Usually, Shaena would've been happy to see a teammate improve so much. But lately all she could do was worry. By the time her head healed, would the team even need her, or would the South Redford Tigers have a new starting post?

"Hey, Shaena," Marisol said quietly, giving her a little nudge. "You okay?"

Yeah, just great, thought Shaena sharply. Aloud, she simply pointed to her head and said, "Headache."

She spent of the rest of the short drive staring out the bus window.

* * *

For the first time since she'd started playing basketball, Shaena was sitting on the bench in her street clothes instead of standing out on the floor in her uniform when the game began. Jessie had started the game in Shaena's place.

The game was another close contest. Rockford was known for their strong defense, and the South players had to mix things up to get an open shot.

At least Marisol was having a great night. After halftime, she stole the ball from a Rockford player just as she was getting ready to shoot. Marisol bolted up the court, dodged two defenders, and went in for a layup. South led by four!

Shaena couldn't help but jump up and cheer along with the rest of the team at Marisol's exciting coast-to-coast move. "Way to go, Mari!" she shouted. Marisol grinned.

Almost absently, Shaena noted that the jumping and cheering didn't make her head hurt.

As the Rockford players took the ball back down the court, Shaena saw Marisol whisper something in Jessie's ear. South had the height advantage with her at post. Jessie stood at least a few inches taller than Rockford's tallest player.

Shaena watched with envy as Jessie got near the basket and used her height to pull down a rebound. She gripped the ball and turned up the court.

Marisol was already sprinting to South's basket. Jessie drew the ball back and threw it as hard as she could in Marisol's direction. Rockford's point guard realized too late what was happening, but she ran to try to catch Marisol anyway. Marisol caught the pass, dribbled once, and scored.

Everyone on the bench jumped up clapping again. South was on fire.

"Amazing pass, Jessie! And great finish, Marisol!" shouted Coach. She turned to Shaena. "That fast-paced offense is exactly what we need to throw off Rockford's defense. Jessie and Marisol are really working well together."

Shaena nodded, but all of the excitement had leaked out of her in a whoosh at the coach's praise. *It looks like the team doesn't need me anymore after all,* she thought bitterly.

She looked up just in time to see Marisol high-fiving Jessie. They were both smiling, eyes shining. They looked like they were having the time of their lives.

Shaena swallowed a lump in her throat. *Maybe Marisol doesn't need me, either.*

South was on fire for the rest of the game, keeping up the fast breaks and aggressive offense. The Rockford coach called a couple of time-outs to try to stop South's momentum, but it was no use. When the final buzzer sounded, South had won with a ten-point lead.

After Coach Riley's post-game talk, Shaena quickly gathered up her things to leave the locker room. She didn't want anyone to see the tears she was struggling to hold back.

But when she turned around, Jessie was standing behind her.

"Hey, Shaena," said Jessie.

"Hey, Jessie," replied Shaena flatly. "Great game."

"Thanks," said Jessie, smiling nervously. "Listen, um, can I ask you something?"

Shaena frowned. "Sure."

"Um . . ." started Jessie, looking at the floor. "Can you give me a few tips sometime? Like on defense? And that drop step move that you do. I can't seem to get the hang of it."

Shaena stared at Jessie. Emotions spun around inside her like a tornado. After the game Jessie had just played, she was asking Shaena for help? Shaena was flattered.

But then she remembered Jessie and Marisol's high five, like they were best friends. Like Jessie was taking her place. That fiery anger flared up in Shaena's chest again. She made her face expressionless.

"Yeah, sure," Shaena replied. "Sometime. You know, when I'm better. But I'm not sure you really need my help. Maybe you should just practice with your best friend Marisol."

Shaena walked past Jessie before the other post player could say anything. As she headed toward the door, she brushed past Marisol.

Marisol turned, her eyes full of concern. "Shaena, wait —"

But Shaena didn't wait. She just walked out of the locker room without another word.

CHAPTER 8

TOUGH TALK

Shaena sat alone at the front of the bus for the trip home. She put in her earphones and pretended to sleep, trying to ignore the chatter of her teammates in the back. When the bus pulled up to the school, she hurried to her mom's car without saying goodbye to anyone.

As they left the parking lot, Shaena felt her phone buzz inside her coat pocket. It was a text from Marisol that simply read, *the park*.

Shaena knew instantly where Marisol meant. There was a park within walking distance of both their houses. It had a small basketball court where Shaena and Marisol had been playing hoops ever since they could dribble a ball.

"Mom, I need to meet Marisol at the park. Please? I don't have any homework or anything," said Shaena.

"Sure, honey," Mom replied. "That sounds like a great idea."

"Really?" asked Shaena. She wasn't usually allowed to go out on school nights.

"Really," her mom confirmed. She was quiet for a moment. "I know it's been hard sitting out this week. If you don't want to talk to me about how you're feeling, talk to Marisol. She's your friend."

Shaena didn't say anything, but she knew her mom was right. She was tired of feeling sad and angry. She couldn't avoid talking to Marisol any longer.

Her mom stopped next to the park. "Call me when you're done," she said. "I'll come get you both for dinner."

Shaena nodded and got out of the car. Marisol hadn't arrived yet, so she sat down on a bench next to the familiar concrete court. After a while, she could see Marisol walking up the sidewalk.

"Hey, Mari. What's up?" Shaena asked quietly when the other girl had reached the court.

Marisol dropped down beside her. "Shaena, what's going on?" she asked.

Shaena cleared her throat. "What do you mean?"

"You've been, like, really mad lately," Marisol started. "You've just been sitting at practice looking grumpy. You won't talk to me or anyone on the team. And I heard what you said to Jessie today in the locker room. That was really mean."

Shaena opened her mouth to tell Marisol that she had it all wrong, but she stopped. Marisol didn't have it all wrong. Shaena was guilty of all of the things her friend had said. But Marisol had no idea what the past week had been like.

"I'm sorry, Mari," Shaena mumbled, pulling up her jacket against the chilly air.

"Okay," said Marisol, sounding frustrated. "But what's going on? Are you mad at me? Are you mad at the team? Please tell me what's bothering you. I miss you."

Shaena looked up in surprise. "What?" she asked.

"I miss playing basketball with you," continued Marisol. "And I miss seeing you happy. I miss my friend."

"Oh," said Shaena. "Well, I . . . I miss you too." She sniffed and then burst into tears.

"Hey, hey," Marisol said, putting a hand on her shoulder. "What is it, Shaena? You can tell me."

The words poured out like a flood. "It's this stupid concussion," Shaena said through her tears.

"I have a headache all the time, and I can't play basketball, and I'm letting down the team, and Jessie is going to take my place on the team and be your best friend."

Shaena broke off, sobbing. She hadn't really realized how much she had kept bottled up these last few days.

"Oh, Shaena," said Marisol, leaning in to give Shaena a hug.

But Shaena drew back — Marisol was smiling! Was she making fun of her?

"Wait, why are you smiling?" asked Shaena.

"Sorry," apologized Marisol, still smiling. "But I need you to listen to me for a second. Are you listening?"

Shaena wiped her eyes and nodded.

"First, I'm so sorry you got a concussion," began Marisol. "But you shouldn't feel ashamed about it. I did some reading about concussions after you got hurt, and —"

Shaena let out a small laugh. "Of course you did." Marisol was always reading up on things. She was like a walking encyclopedia sometimes.

Marisol smiled. "I know — I'm a total nerd. Anyway, I found out concussions are actually a super common injury," she explained. "Especially for athletes. A whole bunch of professional basketball players have had concussions. And some of them couldn't play for weeks!"

"Wow," said Shaena softly. "I didn't know that."

"Me neither," said Marisol. "Now, about this replacing you thing." She looked directly into Shaena's eyes. "Seriously? You've been my best friend since we were two years old. We've been playing HORSE at this park since forever. Right?"

"Right," agreed Shaena.

"And you're a really good basketball player. You work harder than anyone else. And you're *usually* a great teammate," said Marisol with a pointed look.

Shaena hung her head. Marisol was right. She had definitely not been a good teammate lately, especially to Jessie.

"You can't be replaced — not ever," Marisol assured Shaena. "But which do you think would be better for our team — one good post or two good posts playing together?"

Shaena sighed. She *had* been acting silly. "Two good posts?" she asked jokingly.

"Right. Now, please concentrate on getting better so that we can actually *have* two good posts playing together, and maybe we'll have a shot at beating North next week. Got it?" Marisol asked.

Shaena grinned and threw her arms around her best friend. "Got it."

CHAPTER 9

APOLOGIES

"How are you feeling today, Shaena?" Dr. Lee asked on Friday afternoon. She had her flashlight out again and was shining it in and out of Shaena's eyes.

"Good!" Shaena responded happily. "I haven't had a headache in three days. I even got a ten out of ten on my pop quiz in algebra today!"

Even though it had only been a week since she'd gotten her concussion in the Springfield game, to Shaena it had felt like months. She'd gone through the whole school day smiling, excited to finally be returning to the doctor's. She was feeling so much better after talking with Marisol. The only thing still nagging her was how she'd treated Jessie. She couldn't believe she had been so mean.

"That's great," said Dr. Lee. She put the flashlight down. "Now, about your concussion."

Shaena's stomach twisted in anticipation. Would she be returning to the court?

"It looks like you've healed up nicely," the doctor said. "I'm going to release you to play again starting on Monday."

Shaena's heart soared. Finally! She jumped up and hugged Dr. Lee. "Thank you!"

Dr. Lee laughed at Shaena's enthusiasm but then pulled her back. "But if your headache comes back or you feel sick or lightheaded at all, you have to tell your coach or your mom right away. Do you understand?"

"Yes, Dr. Lee," Shaena said. "I promise."

The doctor handed her a note for Coach Riley. "You're ready to start playing again, but you need to be careful," she said. "Concussions are a very common injury, especially for athletes."

Shaena smiled. Marisol had been right, of course!

"And once you've had one concussion, you're more likely to get another," added Dr. Lee. "Especially if you're not fully healed before you start being active. Too many concussions will stop you from ever playing basketball or any other sport."

No more basketball ever? Shaena couldn't stand that thought. "I'll be really careful," she promised.

"Good," replied Dr. Lee. "Then I'll see you again in a week, just for a check-up."

Shaena thanked the doctor again, then hurried her mom out of the clinic and back to the car.

"Mom," she said urgently once they were inside. "You have to take me back to school for practice."

Shaena's mom looked sternly at her. "Dr. Lee said Monday for practice."

"I know," Shaena said. "I won't play, but I really need to talk to Jessie. Please?"

"All right," her mom agreed. "I'll run to the grocery store and then be back right after practice to pick you up."

"Thanks, Mom! You're the best!" Shaena said.

The car came to a stop outside the school's front door. "I'll see you in an hour," Mom said. "And no basketball. Not yet!"

"Yes, Mom," promised Shaena. She had already waited a whole week — a few more days wouldn't be a problem. But this apology couldn't wait.

Shaena got out of the car and walked into school as her mom pulled away. She hurried into the gym. The Tigers were just starting to file out of the locker room to start practice.

Shaena jogged over, looking for Jessie. The other post walked into the gym, chatting with Marisol.

"Hi, Jessie," called Shaena. "I know you have to get out there, but can I talk to you really quick?"

"Hey, Shaena," Jessie said hesitantly. "Sure?" It sounded more like a question, but she came over.

Marisol gave Shaena an encouraging smile. Then she continued to the court with the other players.

"I'm so sorry about yesterday," Shaena started. "I've been selfish, not to mention a jerk. I'd be happy to help you with the drop-step move. Would you mind helping me with that cross-court pass?"

"Oh!" said Jessie, looking surprised. "Yeah. I mean, what?"

"Dealing with the concussion has been really hard, not that that's any excuse for how I've been acting," Shaena explained. "I got worried that you were taking my place, which is totally silly. We're teammates. So now I'm thinking that we can help each other. Then South will have two good post players. We'll be pretty tough to beat!"

Shaena paused and looked at her teammate. "So, is it a deal?" she asked, reaching out her hand.

Jessie grinned and grabbed Shaena's hand. "Deal! Go Tigers!"

CHAPTER 10

REBOUND

Finally, Monday morning rolled around — Shaena could play basketball at last. She had distracted herself all weekend by spending time with Marisol. On Sunday, they had even invited Jessie over to the park. Although Shaena sat on a swing and watched while Marisol and Jessie played some one-on-one, it felt great to just hang out again.

Shaena rushed through her breakfast and quickly got dressed. Even though she had carefully packed her bag for practice the night before, she checked it again to make sure she had everything. Nothing was going to go wrong today.

In the hallway before first hour, Jessie stopped by Shaena's locker. "Hey! Are you ready to play today?" she asked.

"You have no idea!" exclaimed Shaena. "I'm just worried that I won't be able to sit through all of my classes. I can hardly wait."

Jessie laughed. "I'm sure you can make it. See you in practice, and welcome back!"

* * *

Just as Shaena had predicted, her classes crept by at a snail's pace. Earth science took forever, and algebra, as much as she loved it, seemed as though it would never end.

When the last bell finally rang, Shaena nearly knocked her desk over in her rush for the door. In the locker room, she moved faster than anyone else. She was dressed and out on the court before most of her team had even put their shoes on.

Shaena grabbed a ball and shot at a side basket, relishing the feel of the ball spinning in her hands again. There was nothing quite like the *swoosh* of the ball falling through the net.

Coach Riley smiled as soon as she saw Shaena. "I'm so glad you're back, Shaena!" she called, walking over. Shaena had given her Dr. Lee's note at the end of Friday's practice. "I know you're more than ready to play, but we'll take it easy to make sure your headache doesn't come back. It'd be a shame for you to have to sit out again."

"No problem, Coach," said Shaena as she shot another three-pointer. "But I feel great right now."

Coach nodded. "I'm really glad to hear that."

"Shaena!" someone yelled. The rest of the team was filing out of the locker room.

"Oh my gosh! Shaena's back!" shouted Annie. The team cheered and rushed toward Shaena for a group hug.

Shaena smiled as the girls huddled around her. She had missed her team and practice so much. She cleared her throat and said, "You guys? I have something that I'd like to say."

The team looked at her. A lot of the girls looked a bit confused.

"I'm really sorry," Shaena told them. "Ever since I got that concussion, I haven't been a good teammate. And I haven't been a good friend."

"Oh, Shaena. It's okay!" Christine cried out.

"But it's not okay," insisted Shaena. "It wasn't your fault that I couldn't play, but I took my anger out on all of you anyway. It was so hard to just sit on the sidelines. But that's silly and unfair. And I was worried you didn't need me anymore, so I stopped talking to you before you could stop talking to me. That was silly and unfair too. So I'm really sorry. Forgive me?"

"Well," said Annie jokingly. "I suppose . . ."

"I don't know," added Marisol with a smile. "We'll have to see how you do against North first."

The whole team laughed, and Shaena knew everything would be okay again.

"Okay, basketball players!" called Coach, giving a few short claps to get their attention. "Let's start those warm-ups!"

After warm-ups and a quick fast-break drill, Coach split them up into groups by positions so they could work on specific moves. Now was Shaena's chance to help Jessie with her drop step. They took a ball and headed to a side court.

"So when you catch the ball, keep it right at your chin," Shaena told her. "That way, your defender can't poke it out without fouling you."

"That makes sense," said Jessie as she practiced holding the ball just right. "But what I can't seem to get is the angle. When I take the step back, I end up in a weird spot. My shot never goes in!"

"Ooh! I see!" said Shaena. "Instead of stepping straight back, take a big step around your defender's leg. That way you'll have a good angle for the shot, and you'll pin the defender at the same time. Give it a try!"

Jessie followed Shaena's advice and got into position. Shaena had to admit that the other post was a natural. On her first try, Jessie executed the step, dribbled, and shot perfectly.

"Great job, Jessie!" cheered Shaena.

"Thanks! It makes so much more sense now," said Jessie. "I try to watch for it during the games on TV, but the players always move so fast."

"You do that too?" Shaena asked. "I thought I was the only one!"

"Are you kidding? I love watching college basketball and the WNBA," said Jessie. "We should watch together sometime."

"That'd be awesome!" agreed Shaena. "Okay, now that you've mastered the drop step, you have to give me pointers on that cross-court pass."

Shaena grinned as Jessie handed her the ball and started to explain the pass. Marisol was right — two good post players were better than one. She couldn't wait to see what she and Jessie could do during Friday's game.

CHAPTER 11

BACK IN THE GAME

The Friday game against North Redford was at home, and the South Redford Tigers were ready. Practice had gone well all week — Jessie and Shaena had stayed late every night to work together, and the team had never been more in sync.

Now that game day was actually here, though, Shaena was feeling nervous. It wasn't just her normal pregame butterflies, either. She sat on the bench in the locker room and took in big breaths to try to calm her nerves.

"Shaena, are you okay?" someone asked.

Shaena looked over her shoulder to see Jessie coming over to the bench.

"I'm really nervous," Shaena admitted. "I . . . I don't want to get hurt again." She kept thinking about what Dr. Lee had said — that she was more likely to get a concussion now that she'd already had one. "I didn't think about it much this week. But that's because I was just playing with you guys."

"Ugh, I know the feeling," said Jessie as she sat down.

"You do?" asked Shaena.

"Yeah. I broke my finger last season at my old school," said Jessie. She cringed at the memory. "It healed pretty fast, but I was afraid to use that hand for a while."

"How did you stop being afraid?" asked Shaena.

Jessie shrugged. "I just kept playing," she said. "It was only my first season, but I loved basketball right away. Nothing could keep me off the court."

Shaena laughed. She had never realized she and Jessie had so much in common.

"I know the feeling. Thanks for listening, Jessie," said Shaena, standing up. "Now let's go show those North players how South plays basketball!"

* * *

As the two teams got ready for the jump ball, Shaena took her spot. But it wasn't at the center of the court. Jessie was taking the jump ball today.

Shaena didn't mind, though. Jessie was almost as tall as she was and had done a good job in the past game. Shaena also suspected that the coach knew she was feeling a little nervous.

The ref tossed the ball straight up. Jessie jumped and easily won the tip. She landed on the ground with the ball.

"Jessie!" Marisol called. Jessie passed back to Marisol, who started dribbling down the court.

What do I do? Shaena wondered. She was so used to doing the jump ball that she hadn't thought about where to go on the floor.

After a quick decision, she ran to the basket and called to Marisol over her shoulder. Marisol's pass sailed into Shaena's outstretched arms. She took one dribble, then shot.

The ball smacked the backboard and fell back to the floor. She'd missed. Thankfully Christine was there in a flash. She quickly grabbed the rebound and scored.

As Shaena jogged to the other side of the court, Marisol passed her. "You'll get the next one, Shaena," she said.

Shaena wasn't so sure. She never missed layups! A thought passed through her mind. *What if I'm not ready to be back?* But she quickly shook off that idea and focused on the game.

North was one of the toughest teams in the conference, and it showed. They quickly battled back with a long three-pointer, but Annie answered with a three-pointer of her own to put South up by two. The lead teeter-tottered back and forth for a few minutes before Coach Riley signaled to the referee for a time-out.

"Great job out there, team!" she said. "But let's try to slow it down a little bit. North has more players than we do, so we need to conserve our energy."

Shaena nodded, breathing hard. She was already pretty tired, and the game was only a few minutes old. The week off had really affected her endurance.

"Instead of trying to trade more three-pointers with them, let's make that post player of theirs work," Coach continued.

Shaena shot Jessie a grin. This was the chance they'd been waiting for.

* * *

Shaena and Jessie each took their spot on the blocks, just outside of the painted area on either side of the basket. After the time-out, Shaena was feeling pumped and ready to break down North's defense. She knew Jessie and she were ready.

Marisol took the ball and dribbled down the court. She passed to the other guards, Annie and Christine, around the outside. They kept the ball on the perimeter, waiting for North's defense to make a mistake. Soon they did.

Shaena's defender grew impatient and ran to the ball to try to make a play, leaving Shaena unguarded. It was the opening South needed.

"Ball!" called Shaena. Marisol quickly flicked the ball to her.

It zipped straight into Shaena's hands. She turned to shoot, but Jessie's defender had already darted over.

But now Jessie was wide open. "Shaena!" Jessie yelled, her hands out and ready for the ball.

Without hesitation, Shaena passed to the other post. Jessie caught the ball, turned, and took the shot in one smooth motion. The ball rushed through the air — and straight into the net!

"Great shot, Jessie!" Shaena said, giving her a high five as they ran to the other side of the court.

"Great pass!" Jessie returned.

On defense, Shaena and Jessie double-teamed the North post every chance they got. She couldn't score with both girls guarding her, and she couldn't see around them to pass to her team.

During one time-out, Shaena could hear the North post complaining to her teammate.

"I can't do anything with those two around!" she whined as she jogged to the sideline. "I can't see. I can't shoot. What am I supposed to do?"

Shaena felt a little bad for her opponent, but she was happy to hear that their strategy was working. Still, North was a talented team, and they took advantage of every missed shot and turnover South made. At the end of the third quarter, North took the lead after a few expert three-pointers and fast layups.

But South wasn't about to give up. Shaena and Jessie stayed focused, and their teamwork made all the difference. They continued to block the North post, allowing South to step up on offense.

Soon South had taken back the lead. Shaena was having so much fun playing great basketball with Jessie and Marisol, though, that she hardly noticed the score. The clock ticked down until . . .

BUZZZ!

The home crowd in the stands let out a wild cheer. The Tigers had stayed focused and it showed — South was up 43–36. They'd won!

Shaena let out a happy, exhausted sigh as she jogged off the court. She couldn't remember a game ever going by that quickly.

Coach Riley's smile was enormous when she entered the locker room. "Wow. What can I say?

That was a great team effort for a hard-fought win. Shaena and Jessie, your extra work this week really showed," she said. "Fantastic job, everyone."

After the coach had dismissed the team, Marisol came over to Jessie and Shaena. She slung her arms around their tall shoulders.

"Well, after that incredible win, I'm feeling hungry," Marisol told them. "So how about you two MVPs? Are you hungry, Jessie? Because I *know* Shaena's always hungry."

Shaena nodded seriously. "It's true."

Jessie grinned. "I'm starving!"

"Then how about pizza? My house?" Marisol asked.

"Deal!" Jessie and Shaena shouted at the same time, and the three girls burst out laughing.

As they headed out, Shaena couldn't have been happier to be sharing the spotlight with her new teammate — and friend.

ABOUT the AUTHOR

Val Priebe lives in St. Paul, Minnesota, with four dogs, a cat named Cowboy, and a guy named Nick. Val has written several sports books for young readers, including the Sports Illustrated Kids Victory School Superstars series and two Jake Maddox Girl Sport Stories titles, *Full Court Dreams* and *Stolen Bases*. Besides writing books, she loves to spend her time reading, knitting, cooking, and coaching basketball.

GLOSSARY

aching (AKE-ing) — full of dull pain that won't go away

concentrate (KAHN-suhn-trayt) — to focus your thoughts and attention on something

concussion (kuhn-KUH-shuhn) — a brain injury that happens when your brain knocks against the inside of your skull, usually from a hard blow to the head

conditioning (kuhn-DISH-uh-ning) — the process of becoming stronger and healthier through exercise

dazed (DAYZD) — stunned and unable to think clearly

defiantly (di-FYE-uhnt-lee) — done in a way that purposefully disobeys something or someone

momentum (moh-MEN-tuhm) — the continuing strength or force of something

strategies (STRAT-uh-jeez) — careful plans or methods

symptoms (SIMP-tuhmz) — signs that suggest a person is sick or has a health problem

wincing (WINSS-ing) — flinching or pulling back in pain or embarrassment

DISCUSSION QUESTIONS

1. Talk about why Shaena was acting mean toward her friends and teammates. Look back at the text and then explain her reasons in your own words.

2. Because sports are physical activities, injuries sometimes happen. There are ways to play safely so that you can lower the risk of getting hurt, however. Talk about what you could do to avoid getting injured while playing sports. If you have time, trying researching sports safety and compare your answers.

3. In the story, we find out a lot about how Shaena felt. How do you think Jessie felt throughout the story? How about Marisol? What in the text makes you think that?

WRITING PROMPTS

1. Have you ever had to sit out of an activity or miss something because you were sick or injured? Write two paragraphs about how you felt and how you handled the situation.

2. Shaena had a hard time sitting out of basketball for a week. Write one paragraph that explains why she needed to follow the doctor's instructions, and then write a second paragraph suggesting what she could've done while healing to still feel like a part of the team.

3. Using examples from the book, write two paragraphs about why Shaena's attitude changed. What caused her to switch from feeling sad and angry to feeling happy again?

-MOVES-

Basketball has many types of passes, shots, and plays. Read about a few used in the story!

Double team — when two players temporarily guard one opponent

Fast break — a type of play where a defensive player grabs a rebound, then passes the ball down the court to a teammate for a quick shot before the other team has a chance to defend their basket

Guarding — when a player tries to keep an opponent from receiving the ball, making a shot, or passing to another player

Inbound pass — a pass that puts the ball back inbounds and starts play again

Layup — a shot taken close to the basket after dribbling, usually shot with one hand and with one foot in the air

Rebound — when a player grabs a ball that is coming off the rim or backboard after an unsuccessful shot

-POSITIONS-

There are no regulated positions in basketball, and the terms have changed over the years. Here are some of the more common terms:

The **point guard** directs the team on the court and sets up plays, usually staying farther from the basket. She has excellent ball handling and passing skills.

When a team needs to score a lot of points, they rely on their **shooting guard**. Like the point guard, a shooting guard plays away from the basket but is more focused on offense and scoring.

The **power forward** plays close to the basket and isn't afraid to go in for rebounds or block her opponent's shots. She also scores close to the basket.

One of the most versatile players on the team is the **small forward**. She can shoot and defend really well, and she can play next to the basket or farther back.

The **center** is often the tallest player. On defense, she uses her height to block shots and grab rebounds. On offense, she makes shots close to the basket.

A **post player** stays close to the basket. She plays with her back to the net as she defends or as she waits for a pass from a guard. Both centers and power forwards are sometimes called post players.

THE FUN DOESN'T STOP HERE!

FIND MORE AT:
CAPSTONEKIDS.com

Authors and Illustrators | Videos and Contests
Games and Puzzles | Heroes and Villains

Find cool websites and
more books like this one at
www.facthound.com

Just type in the Book ID:
9781496531667
and you're ready to go!